USBORNE WORLD WILDLIFE

GRASSLAND WILDLIFE

Kamini Khanduri

Designed by Andrew Dixon
Illustrated by Ian Jackson

Series editor: Felicity Brooks
Scientific consultant: David Duthie
Map illustrations by Janos Marffy

Contents

Grassland areas

Grasslands are large, open areas of land, covered in grass. Low bushes and a few trees may also grow there. Today, many grassland areas are used by people as farmland, but in places where people do not farm, grasslands are home to lots of different kinds of wild plants and animals. The big picture below shows a hot African grassland, and some of the exciting wildlife that lives there.

Fires in grasslands are often started by sparks of lightning during storms. When it has not rained for a long time, the grass, bushes and trees are very dry, so they catch fire easily and burn quickly.

Trees and grasses

Trees need a lot of water. There is not much rain in grassland areas so most species (kinds) of trees cannot grow there. The few trees which do grow have special ways of surviving at dry times of the year.

Baobab tree with swollen trunk

Whenever it rains, baobab trees take up lots of water from the soil. They store the water inside their trunks which look very swollen.

Grasses do not need as much water as taller plants, so about 10,000 different species grow in grasslands. These three species grow in North America.

Buffalo grass

Big bluestem grass

Little bluestem grass

Acacia tree

Trees provide food and shelter for animals.

Giraffes

Cattle egrets

Buffaloes

Elephants

When it has not rained for a long time, animals gather at areas of water, called waterholes. These may be very far apart.

Many plant-eating animals, such as zebras and antelopes, live in groups. They are safer from enemies if they stay together.

Zebras

Antelopes

Puff adder

Reptiles, such as snakes and lizards, live among the grasses, or on rocks.

Grasslands of the world

Grasslands cover about a quarter of the world. This map shows where they are. There are two kinds of grassland areas - tropical and temperate. In tropical areas, it is hot all year long with two seasons - a rainy one and a dry one. In temperate areas, there are four seasons, with hot summers and cold winters.

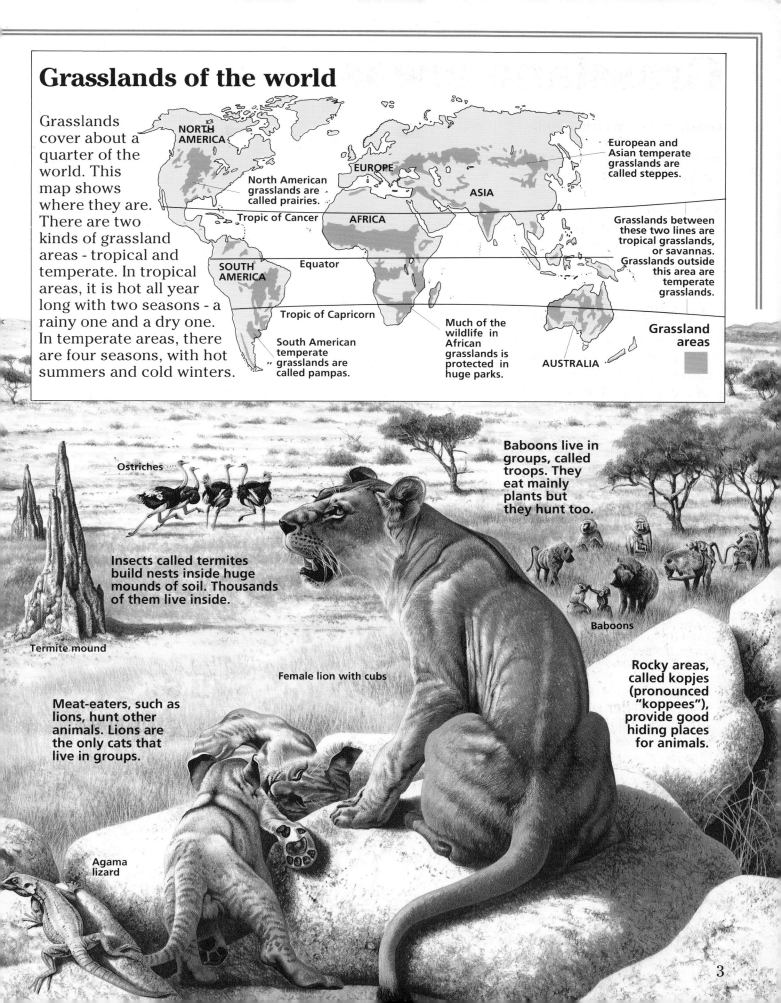

NORTH AMERICA

EUROPE

ASIA

AFRICA

SOUTH AMERICA

AUSTRALIA

North American grasslands are called prairies.

European and Asian temperate grasslands are called steppes.

Tropic of Cancer

Equator

Tropic of Capricorn

South American temperate grasslands are called pampas.

Much of the wildlife in African grasslands is protected in huge parks.

Grasslands between these two lines are tropical grasslands, or savannas. Grasslands outside this area are temperate grasslands.

Grassland areas

Ostriches

Baboons live in groups, called troops. They eat mainly plants but they hunt too.

Insects called termites build nests inside huge mounds of soil. Thousands of them live inside.

Baboons

Termite mound

Female lion with cubs

Rocky areas, called kopjes (pronounced "koppees"), provide good hiding places for animals.

Meat-eaters, such as lions, hunt other animals. Lions are the only cats that live in groups.

Agama lizard

Plant-eaters

All kinds of animals feed on the grasses, bushes and trees that grow in grasslands. Plant-eating animals are called herbivores. They have to eat more often than meat-eaters because plants do not contain as much nourishment as meat. Many herbivores spend almost all day feeding, or looking for food.

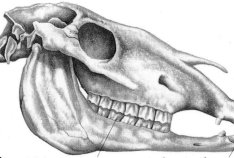

Molar teeth are used for grinding and chewing.

Incisor teeth are used for cutting and gnawing.

This picture shows a zebra's skull. Like most herbivores, zebras have strong teeth to cut and grind tough plants.

Kangaroos

Kangaroos live in Australian grasslands, in groups called mobs. There are 14 different species. Instead of running, kangaroos jump along on their back legs, using their tails to help them balance. When they are feeding, they lean forward onto all fours and move slowly along. They usually feed during the night and grasses are their main food. Kangaroos are marsupials (animals that carry their babies in pouches). Baby kangaroos are called joeys.

This female grey kangaroo is carrying her baby in her pouch. The baby feeds on milk from a nipple inside the pouch.

Babies that have left the pouch jump back in if there is danger.

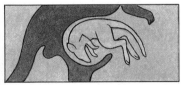

They jump in head first so their tails and back feet are sticking out.

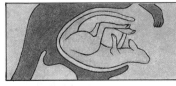

Then they turn around inside the pouch and poke their heads out too.

Short front legs

Baby peeping out of pouch

Long, heavy tail helps the kangaroo balance.

Long, strong back legs for jumping

Food for all

Different herbivores feed on different plants, or on different parts of the same plant. This means that more species can live in one area without competing for food. Animals that feed on grasses are called grazers. Animals that feed on bushes or trees are called browsers. Some animals are both grazers and browsers. The animals in this picture live in African savannas. (They would not really be found so close together.)

Elephants stretch their trunks up to browse on leaves, twigs and branches. They also reach down to the ground to pull up grasses.

Gerenuks, a species of antelope, can stand up on their back legs to browse on leaves from bushes.

Warthogs pluck short grasses with their teeth and lips.

Giraffes have long necks so they can browse on the top parts of trees. They pull off leaves and twigs with their lips and tongues.

Male giraffes stretch up to reach leaves above their heads.

Female giraffes browse on leaves just below their mouths.

Black rhinos browse on leaves from bushes at the same level as their heads.

Dik-diks, the smallest antelopes, browse on the lowest parts of bushes.

Rodents

Rodents have long, sharp incisor teeth so they can gnaw through very tough plants. Many species of rodents live in grasslands. They often live in large groups. (These pictures are not to scale.)

Maras live in South American pampas.

Gophers live in North American prairies.

Naked mole-rats live in burrows in African savannas.

Susliks live in Asian steppes.

Antelopes

Antelopes are related to deer. About 50 species live in grasslands, or feed there during part of the year. Some are grazers and some are browsers. Most can run very fast to escape from enemies. All the antelopes shown here live in African savannas, except for the pronghorn which lives in North American prairies, and the saiga which lives in Asian steppes.

Klipspringer

Thomson's gazelle

Grant's gazelle

Saiga

Impala

Springbok

Pronghorn

Bontebok

Kob

Blesbok

Topi

Waterbuck

Wildebeest

Hartebeest

Common eland

Roan antelope

Problems for plants

The leaves of grassland plants are always being eaten by animals. Grasses are better at surviving this than trees. They have long, straight leaves that grow upward from the bottom of the plant. The tops of the leaves are eaten, but the growing parts near the ground are left untouched.

When an animal bites off grass leaves from the top, the leaves keep growing from the bottom. In time, the same leaves grow tall again.

When an animal feeds on a tree's leaves, it eats the whole leaf, including the growing part, so the tree has to grow new leaves. Some trees have ways of protecting their leaves from animals.

Acacia trees have long, spiky thorns on their branches. This stops some animals from eating their leaves. Some species of acacias also have nasty-tasting leaves.

Elephants sometimes destroy whole trees while they are feeding.

Elephants

Elephants are the largest land animals. They can live for up to 60 years and have an amazing ability to learn and remember things. On African savannas, elephants live in family groups. They travel long distances each day, in search of food, water and shady trees. They need to eat a lot, because they are so big. All the elephants in this book are African elephants.

Female African elephant

An elephant's tusks are long incisor teeth. They first appear at around the age of two and go on growing all through the elephant's life. Elephants use their tusks to scrape bark off trees and to dig for roots.

Baby African elephant

Hyraxes are related to elephants, although they look nothing like them. They are about the size of big rabbits and they live on kopjes.

Baby elephants are called calves. They are usually very playful. They feed on their mother's milk until they are three or four years old.

Useful noses

An elephant's trunk is its nose. There are two nostrils at the end of it. Trunks are very useful.

Two "lips" at the end of the trunk are used like fingers to pick things up and to pluck grass.

Elephants suck water into their trunks and squirt it into their mouths or over their bodies.

When they meet, elephants often touch each other with their trunks, as a greeting.

Mothers often stroke their babies with their trunks, and gently guide them along.

Meat-eaters

Animals that eat meat are called carnivores. Carnivores that hunt other animals are called predators and the animals they hunt are called prey. Most predators have sharp eyesight and hearing, and a good sense of smell. Wherever they live, carnivores depend on other animals for food. The animals they eat may be carnivores themselves, or herbivores. One way of showing who eats what in a particular area is by a food web. The picture below shows part of a food web in a North American prairie. (The pictures are not to scale.)

Lions have teeth that are well-suited to eating meat. They kill prey with their long canine teeth and slice it up with their sharp molar teeth.

An arrow from one thing to another means the first is eaten by the second. For example, mice are eaten by skunks, and skunks are eaten by golden eagles.

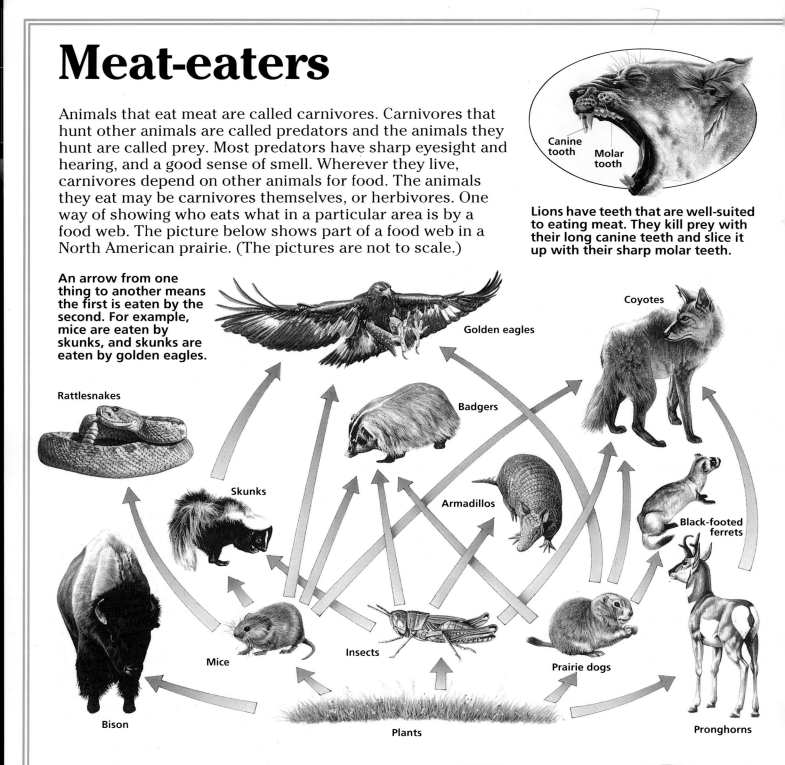

Canine tooth   Molar tooth

Golden eagles

Coyotes

Rattlesnakes

Badgers

Skunks

Armadillos

Black-footed ferrets

Mice

Insects

Prairie dogs

Bison

Plants

Pronghorns

Hunting in burrows

In temperate grasslands, many small animals live underground. They run into their burrows when they see a predator approaching. During the winter, they may not come out at all. Some predators can find these animals even inside their burrows. They have to use their sense of smell because it is too dark to see clearly.

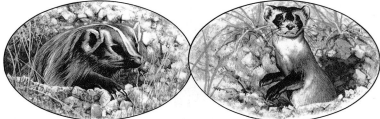

American badgers dig out small animals, such as mice and prairie dogs, from their burrows.

Black-footed ferrets chase prairie dogs into their burrows and hunt them underground.

Wild dogs

African wild dogs live in groups, called packs, of up to 30 members. They travel over huge areas in search of food. They hunt in the cool early morning or in the evening shade, feeding mainly on Thomson's gazelles, wildebeest and zebras. The whole pack hunts together, working as a team. This means they can catch larger prey than a single dog could. These pictures show a pack of dogs hunting wildebeest.

The dogs spot the wildebeest from a distance and approach slowly at first.

The wildebeest scatter in all directions as soon as they see the dogs. Most of them manage to escape.

The dogs start to run. They can run fast - up to 70kph (44mph).

Early in the hunt, the dogs pick one of the wildebeest to chase - usually a young, old or sick animal.

When the dogs catch the wildebeest, they attack it from underneath.

After killing the wildebeest, all the dogs share the meal. The older dogs usually let the younger ones feed first.

Cheetahs

Cheetahs live in African savannas. The females live alone except when they have babies. The males often live in small groups of two or three. Cheetahs can run at speeds of up to 110kph (68mph) and are the world's fastest land animals. They hunt alone during the day, feeding mainly on Thomson's gazelles. Although they can run fast, they cannot keep up this speed for long, so they stalk their prey for up to three hours before starting to chase it. Only about half their chases are successful.

Cheetahs often climb up onto termite mounds to get a better view of the area around them. They have excellent eyesight.

This cheetah is stalking a gazelle. If the gazelle looks up, the cheetah stops and stands absolutely still. The gazelle cannot easily see it among the tall grasses.

When it is about 30m (100ft) from the gazelle, the cheetah springs forward into a run. The gazelle runs too. The chase hardly ever lasts longer than a minute.

If it catches up with the gazelle, the cheetah trips it over with its paw and kills it by biting its throat. Then it drags it away to a hiding place before eating it.

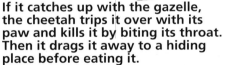

Small, rounded head

Small, flattish ears

Cheetah cubs

Cheetahs usually have three babies at a time. Baby cheetahs, called cubs, are very playful. They climb around and even jump onto their mother's back. Cubs stay with their mother for about 18 months.

Female cheetah

Cheetahs are slim, graceful cats with strong muscles and long legs. They have small, round, black spots on their coats and black stripes running down the sides of their noses.

Storing food

Predators often cannot eat the whole of a kill at once. Some species hide the remains of their food, or store it where other animals cannot get to it. They return to these hiding places when they are hungry again.

Hyenas often hide their leftover food in holes in the ground or muddy pools.

Leopards drag their prey up into trees. They eat what they can and store the remains among the branches.

Scavengers

Carnivores do not always kill their own food. Sometimes they feed on animals that have been killed by other animals, or have died naturally. This is called scavenging. It means that nothing is wasted and the ground is kept clear of carcasses (the bodies of dead animals). Many predators, such as lions and wild dogs, often scavenge too. The picture below shows hyenas, jackals and vultures scavenging on a zebra carcass. Vultures get nearly all their food by scavenging. Different species feed in different ways.

Lappet-faced vultures are very strong, with big, sharp beaks. They can rip up tough skin and muscle that other species cannot feed on.

White-backed vultures stick their heads right inside a carcass to feed. The feathers on their heads are short so they do not get too dirty.

Egyptian vultures stand away from the carcass, waiting to feed on scraps of food that have been torn off and tossed aside by larger species.

Hyenas have strong jaws to crack open bones and feed on the marrow inside.

Spotted hyena

Egyptian vultures

Lappet-faced vulture

Vultures are often the first to spot a dead animal. They see it from the sky and fly down immediately.

Hyenas and jackals get some of their food by scavenging but they often hunt too.

White-backed vulture

Zebra carcass

Golden jackal

A group of scavengers may take only a few minutes to finish a carcass, leaving nothing but a pile of bones.

11

The changing seasons

During the dry season in tropical grasslands, areas of water dry up, trees lose their leaves and grasses stop growing. Some animals have to travel long distances to find food and water. These journeys are called migrations. The most spectacular migrations are those of wildebeest and zebras in the Serengeti National Park in Tanzania, Africa.

Wildebeest

Zebras

Up to a million wildebeest and thousands of zebras migrate together. Their trampling hoofs make paths in the soil.

Animals may have to swim across rivers on their journey. They usually cross at the same place each year. Some animals drown and some are eaten by crocodiles.

Nile crocodile

Migration routes

The map below shows the migration routes of animals in the Serengeti National Park. Thomson's gazelles migrate with wildebeest and zebras. These three species eat different parts of the same grasses, so they can feed in the same area without competing for food.

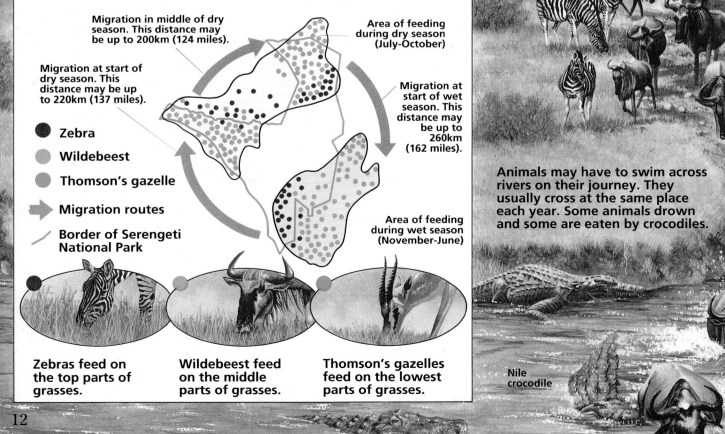

Migration in middle of dry season. This distance may be up to 200km (124 miles).

Area of feeding during dry season (July-October)

Migration at start of dry season. This distance may be up to 220km (137 miles).

Migration at start of wet season. This distance may be up to 260km (162 miles).

- ● Zebra
- ● Wildebeest
- ● Thomson's gazelle
- ➜ Migration routes
- ⟋ Border of Serengeti National Park

Area of feeding during wet season (November-June)

Zebras feed on the top parts of grasses.

Wildebeest feed on the middle parts of grasses.

Thomson's gazelles feed on the lowest parts of grasses.

12

Rainy days

At the start of the rainy season, dark clouds fill the sky. There is often lightning too.

Rain begins to fall, making pools of water on the dry ground. It rains for about two months.

Pools of water join together into lakes or marshy areas. Animals come to drink or play there.

After the rain, the grasses start to grow again and the trees grow new leaves.

In some years, called drought years, there is no rain. Thousands of animals may die of thirst or hunger.

Predators, such as hyenas, often follow migrating herds for part of their journey. They usually catch old, young or weak animals.

Spotted hyenas

White-backed vultures

Migrating animals may travel as far as 1,609km (1,000 miles) a year, and up to 80km (50 miles) in one day.

Hard winters

In temperate grasslands, the winters can be bitterly cold. Small animals burrow underground and stay there until spring. Larger animals have to survive in the open air. The ground is often covered with up to 50cm (20in) of snow and the temperature may be well below freezing point.

Bison have thick, shaggy coats to keep them warm. They dig under the snow, searching for plants.

Avoiding enemies

There are not many hiding places on grasslands, so animals have to find other ways of avoiding their enemies. Small animals, such as rodents, usually try to run into their burrows if there is danger. Very large animals, such as elephants and rhinos, are safe from most predators because of their size. Other animals have different ways of avoiding enemies.

Keeping a look-out

Animals have to look out for enemies all the time, to avoid being taken by surprise. This is easier for animals that live in groups. Together, they have more eyes, ears and noses to sense danger. In some species, such as dwarf mongooses, group members take turns as look-outs. If there is danger, the look-out gives loud warning calls and the rest of the group runs to hide.

Most herbivores have eyes on the sides of their heads, so they can see all around even while they are feeding with their heads down.

Dwarf mongoose

Dwarf mongooses often stand on termite mounds to look out for enemies. They have a better view from higher up.

Running away

Running away is the most common way of escaping from enemies.

Kangaroos jump along at speeds of up to 50kph (30mph).

Ostriches run along at speeds of up to 80kph (50mph).

Gazelles gallop along at speeds of up to 100kph (60mph).

Warning signals

Some animals give warning signals if they are in danger. This can let other members of their group know about the danger. It can also confuse an enemy so that it does not attack.

As they run, pronghorns fluff up the white hairs on their rumps. This flashes a warning to the rest of the herd.

Skunks warn enemies away by stamping their feet and raising their tails. If this does not work, they squirt them with a nasty-smelling liquid from under their tails.

Striped skunk

Springboks pronking

Springboks leap high into the air, arching their backs and landing on all four feet at once. This is called pronking. It shows an enemy how fit they are and may stop it from attacking.

Camouflage

Many animals match their surroundings. This is called camouflage. A lot of grassland animals are brown with stripes or patches, so they blend with grasses and bushes. If a camouflaged animal keeps still, predators cannot easily spot it.

Mound of earth

Young saiga antelope

If they crouch on the ground and keep very still, young saiga antelopes look like mounds of earth. They do this when there is danger.

Fighting back

Instead of hiding or running away, some animals fight back, or turn to face their enemies.

Buffaloes facing an enemy

Buffaloes stand in a line, with their fierce-looking horns facing the enemy. The babies are protected between the adults.

Adult giraffes are safe from most predators because of their size, but babies are sometimes attacked. Mother giraffes protect their babies by kicking out at predators.

Giraffe kicking lion

Insects

These pages show some of the more unusual insects living in grasslands. Many common insects, such as ants, bees, wasps, butterflies and grasshoppers, live there too. Some insects eat plants and some bite other animals to feed on their blood. Many insects stay hidden in the soil, or among the grasses. Although they are small, insects are very important. The tiny tsetse fly in Africa is the main reason why people do not live or farm in some savanna areas.

When tsetse flies bite people or farm animals, they can give them diseases. Wild animals do not get these diseases.

Beetle balls

Dung beetles gather the dung (droppings) of other animals. Some species make the dung into balls. If a male and female beetle meet at a pile of dung, the male makes a ball. Then the two of them roll the ball as far as 15m (50ft). They eat some of the dung and bury the rest in their underground burrow. Then the female lays her eggs in it.

These two dung beetles are rolling a ball of dung. The male is pushing from one side and the female is pulling from the other.

Female dung beetle pulling with front legs

Ball of dung

Male dung beetle pushing with back legs

In some species, the female beetle rides on top of the ball while the male pushes.

Termite homes

Termites live mainly in tropical grasslands. Many species build nests inside huge mounds which they make out of soil, saliva and droppings. In each nest, there is one queen termite, one king termite and lots of soldiers and workers. Each type has a different job.

Tower

Queen's chamber

Inside the nest, there are lots of chambers (rooms), joined by tunnels. Tall, hollow towers up to 7.6m (25ft) high let fresh air in and stale air out.

Queen

The king and queen are the parents of all the other termites. The queen's body is so big, she cannot move at all.

The queen lays eggs all the time - up to 36,000 a day. The workers carry the eggs away to the nursery chambers.

The eggs hatch into tiny white larvae (young). The workers look after them. The larvae grow up to be workers or soldiers.

To feed the termites, the workers grow fungus in garden chambers. They also gather grass from outside the nest.

The soldiers have sharp jaws and huge heads, like helmets. They protect the nest from enemies, such as ants.

Swarming locusts

Locusts are a kind of grasshopper. They have strong jaws to chew tough leaves. When it rains, huge numbers swarm together to feed. There may be 1,000 million locusts in a swarm and each may eat its own weight in food every day. In farming areas, locusts do a lot of damage to crops.

Female locusts stretch the egg-laying part of their bodies to about twice its normal length, to lay their eggs deep in the soil.

Stretched part of locust's body

Eggs inside foamy liquid

Insect-eaters

These animals eat almost nothing but insects. They eat mainly ants and termites and can destroy whole nests.

Aardvark

Giant anteater

Giant anteaters live mainly in South America. They lick up termites with their long, sticky tongues.

Aardvarks live in Africa. To feed, they push their long snouts into termite nests. They feed alone at night.

Armadillo

Armadillos live in North and South America. Their bodies are covered in hard, bony plates. These protect them from enemies.

Bat-eared foxes live in Africa. Their huge ears help them hear termites moving underground.

Bat-eared fox

Birds

Many different kinds of birds live in grasslands. Most birds feed on seeds or insects, so there is usually plenty of food for them there. Birds of prey, such as eagles and falcons, feed on other birds or on small animals, such as mice and other rodents. These pictures show some of the birds found in grasslands around the world.

Little bustard

Ground hornbill

Prairie falcon

Yellow-bellied sunbird

Prairie chicken

Budgerigar

Crested tinamou

Sulphur-crested cockatoo

Horned lark

Golden eagle

Meadow pipit

Saddlebill stork

Secretary bird

Pink-breasted galah

Emu

Black-necked screamer

Crowned crane

Bateleur eagle

Rhea

Lilac-breasted roller

Superb starling

Unusual feeders

Some birds feed on unusual types of food, or have unusual ways of getting their food.

Rufous-backed shrike

Some species of shrikes spike their prey onto thorns after they have killed it. This holds the prey firm while the shrike feeds on it.

Egyptian vultures

Locust stuck onto acacia thorn by shrike

Egyptian vultures break ostrich eggs by dropping stones onto them. Then they feed on the insides.

Helping each other

Small birds are often found on or near larger animals. Sometimes the bird is useful to the larger animal, sometimes the larger animal is useful to the bird and sometimes the two help each other.

Oxpeckers on buffalo

Oxpeckers feed on insects that live on or under the skin of larger animals. These animals would not be able to remove the insects themselves.

Cattle egrets feed on insects that have been disturbed by the feet of larger animals. If they sense danger, the birds fly into the air, calling and warning the larger animal.

Cattle egrets with elephant

African honey guides are birds which feed on wax from bees' nests. They cannot open the nests themselves so they guide people, or other animals that eat honey, to the nest. These pictures show a honey guide leading a honey badger to a bees' nest.

The honey guide calls loudly and flutters around from tree to tree to attract the attention of the honey badger.

The badger follows the bird along. When the bird stops and falls silent, the badger looks for a bees' nest.

When the badger finds the nest, it tears it open and eats the honey. Then the bird flies down and eats the wax.

Courtship

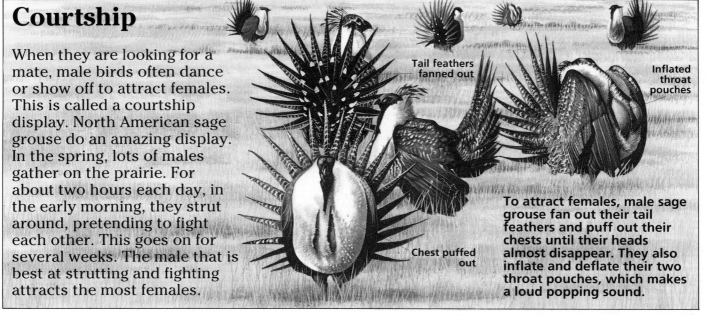

When they are looking for a mate, male birds often dance or show off to attract females. This is called a courtship display. North American sage grouse do an amazing display. In the spring, lots of males gather on the prairie. For about two hours each day, in the early morning, they strut around, pretending to fight each other. This goes on for several weeks. The male that is best at strutting and fighting attracts the most females.

Tail feathers fanned out

Inflated throat pouches

Chest puffed out

To attract females, male sage grouse fan out their tail feathers and puff out their chests until their heads almost disappear. They also inflate and deflate their two throat pouches, which makes a loud popping sound.

Ostriches

Ostriches live in African savannas. They are the biggest birds in the world and can be up to 2.5m (8ft) tall - taller than a horse. Ostriches cannot fly, but they can run very fast to escape from predators. They feed mainly on grass and other plants. Both the males and the females look after the chicks.

Ostriches are so tall, they can see over the tops of bushes and long grass. This helps them to spot predators. They also have excellent eyesight.

Male ostrich

Long neck

Female ostrich

Ostrich chicks are speckled and striped. This helps them to stay hidden among the grass.

Ostrich chicks

Long, powerful legs help ostriches to run fast.

Ostriches only have two toes on each foot. Most birds have four.

To attract females, a male ostrich leans his head back and moves it quickly from side to side. He beats his wings and flutters his tail.

The male may mate with several females which all lay their eggs in one nest on the ground. Ostrich eggs are about 15cm (6 inches) long.

The male and one of the females take turns keeping the eggs warm. Eggs at the edge of the nest that are left uncovered get cold and do not hatch.

After about a month, chicks hatch out of the eggs. They can run almost immediately and both parents protect them from predators.

20

Safe nests

Because there are so few trees in grasslands, it is difficult for birds to find nesting places. Lots of birds of the same species may make their nests in one tree. Some birds make their nests on the ground. They have to guard their eggs and chicks carefully, so predators do not steal them. Some birds have ways of making safe nests.

Rufous ovenbird on nest

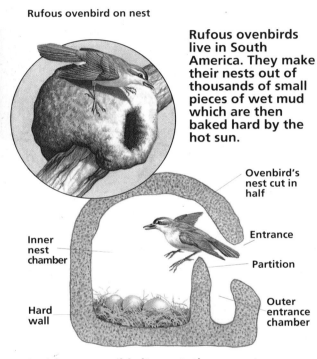

Rufous ovenbirds live in South America. They make their nests out of thousands of small pieces of wet mud which are then baked hard by the hot sun.

Ovenbird's nest cut in half

Inner nest chamber

Entrance

Partition

Hard wall

Outer entrance chamber

Inside an ovenbird's nest, there are two chambers with a partition between them. The ovenbirds can just fit over the top of the partition but larger predators cannot get into the nest chamber.

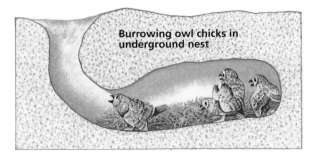

Burrowing owl chicks in underground nest

Burrowing owls live in North and South America. They make their nests in underground burrows. If a predator, such as a coyote, approaches, the owls make hissing noises. The coyote thinks there are snakes in the burrow and does not attack.

Amazing weavers

Weaverbirds make very complicated nests out of lots of pieces of grass. Different species make different shapes but the nests usually hang from a branch. It is the male that makes the nest.

The male weaverbird gathers long strips of grass and uses his beak and feet to knot them onto twigs.

He weaves in more grass, until he has made a hanging circle. He then builds the rest of the nest outward from this circle, leaving an entrance hole underneath or at the front.

The male hangs upside down from the finished nest, flapping his wings and calling to attract a female. If no female is happy with his nest, the male destroys it and starts all over again.

Social weaverbirds' nests

Social weaverbirds build their nests side by side, with one roof over all of them. There may be 30 nests under one roof, each with its own entrance underneath. Sometimes the nest is so heavy, it breaks the branches that support it.

Living in groups

Many animals live in groups instead of by themselves. The members of a group may feed together, look after each other's babies and groom each other. Groups of predators often hunt together, so they can catch bigger prey. In larger groups, the members may come and go. In smaller groups, they may stay together for longer, like a family.

These female zebras are grooming each other. They use their teeth to pick dirt, insects and bits of grass out of each other's fur.

Elephant families

Female elephants and their young live in family groups of up to 30. There is a very strong bond between the members of a family. If one elephant is injured, the others help it. If it dies, they get very upset and may stay with the body for hours. A scientist called Cynthia Moss has been studying the elephants in Amboseli National Park in Kenya since 1973. She can recognize nearly all the 650 elephants that live there and has learned a lot about how a family behaves.

Matriarch

The whole family helps to look after the babies.

The oldest female, called the matriarch, is the leader. As she leads her family around, they learn about the area where they live.

The adult females are either sisters or daughters of the matriarch.

When young females become adults, some leave to start new families.

Males leave the family when they are about 14. Adult males usually live alone.

▼ Adult female
▽ Young male
▽ Young female
▽ Baby

Fighting

Animals that live in groups are not always peaceful. Sometimes they fight each other. Pairs of males have fights over females, or to protect a particular area. In most species, the females do not fight.

Kangaroos hold each other with their front legs and kick with their back legs.

Bison put their heads together and push hard against each other.

Young giraffes use their necks to push each other slowly from side to side.

Prairie dog towns

Prairie dogs are rodents, not dogs. They get their name because they make barking noises. They live in underground burrows in family groups, called coteries. Areas where there are lots of coteries are called prairie dog towns. Today, many of these areas have been taken over by farmers, so numbers of prairie dogs are much lower than they used to be.

Adults take turns as look-outs. If there is danger, they whistle and the whole family scurries underground.

When two prairie dogs meet, they often touch noses, or "kiss", as a greeting.

Both males and females help look after the young.

Prairie dogs feed on grasses. They keep the grass around their burrows short, so they have a good view of the surrounding area.

Prairie dogs build mounds of soil around their burrow entrances. This helps stop water from getting in and flooding the burrow.

In the burrow

Inside their burrows, prairie dogs are protected from most enemies, and from the cold in winter. No two burrows are exactly the same. Like people, prairie dogs often make changes to their home. They dig new tunnels and block up old ones. A burrow may have several entrances and lots of different chambers. If it gets too crowded, some of the prairie dogs leave to dig new burrows.

Entrance

Chamber for listening for enemies above ground

Black-footed ferret chasing prairie dog down burrow

Chamber for hiding from ferrets

Rattlesnake sheltering in prairie dog burrow

Chamber for sheltering when the rest of the burrow is flooded

Nest chamber

Prairie dog digging a new tunnel

Unused tunnel blocked up with soil or droppings

Caring for young

Mammals are animals that give birth to live babies, instead of laying eggs. They feed their babies with their own milk for the first part of their lives. This is called suckling. Most newborn baby mammals cannot look after themselves. In some species, they become independent very quickly but in others, the mother looks after them for a long time. Many mammals carry their babies around when they are little.

Baboons

Baby baboons are born with black fur which turns brown as they get older. They can walk at about a week old, but their mothers carry them when they are moving far. All the members of a baboon troop help to look after the babies. They play with them and groom them.

Baby baboon

For its first few months, a baby baboon clings to the long hair on its mother's belly as she carries it around.

At about three months, a baby baboon can ride on its mother's back. When the mother runs, the baby lies flat and holds on tight.

Female olive baboon grooming her baby

Tiny kangaroos

Newborn kangaroos are only about 2.5cm (1 inch) long and weigh less than one gram (0.04oz). Immediately after being born, they climb 15cm (6 inches) to their mother's pouch, where they keep on growing.

The baby kangaroo makes its way up the front of its mother's body, pulling itself along with its front legs.

When it reaches the pouch, it crawls in and finds a nipple. It stays there feeding and growing for about six months.

Even after leaving the pouch, the baby returns to feed. It sucks from the same nipple it used when it was in the pouch.

A mother kangaroo may feed two babies at once - one tiny one inside the pouch and one bigger one outside.

Baby food

When suckling stops, baby mammals have to find food. Herbivores follow their mother around, feeding on plants when she feeds. In some species of predators, the adults feed first and then regurgitate (bring up) some of their food for their babies to eat. They do this until the babies can hunt for themselves.

Mother cheetahs sometimes catch baby gazelles and give them to their cubs so they can try out their hunting skills.

Cheetah cub chasing baby gazelle

Hiding from enemies

One of the greatest dangers for baby animals is being caught and eaten by other animals. Predators often attack babies - even those of species that they would not attack as adults. Babies are easier to catch because they are smaller and weaker and they cannot run very fast. Many animals have ways of hiding their babies from predators.

Wild dogs sometimes move their pups from one den to another so predators, such as hyenas, cannot find them so easily.

Wild dog moving pup to a new den

Pronghorns hide their fawns in long grass while they feed nearby. Fawns only spend about 20 minutes a day with their mothers.

Pronghorn fawn hiding in grass

The birth of a zebra

A female zebra lies on the ground to give birth. The baby, which is called a foal, comes out front feet first.

The birth takes about seven minutes. The mother lifts her head and licks her newborn foal to clean its fur.

Less than five minutes later, the foal tries to stand. At first, its legs are very wobbly and it keeps falling over.

When the foal has managed to stand without falling, it feeds on its mother's milk. This makes it stronger.

15 minutes after being born, the foal joins the rest of the zebra herd, ready to run with them if predators attack.

Snakes

Snakes are reptiles - animals with dry, scaly skins. The largest grassland species is the African rock python which can be up to 9m (30ft) long. All snakes are carnivores. Although they have no legs, they can move quickly to chase their prey. They usually slither along on the ground, but some species climb trees too.

Sac containing poison

Fang

Tube for carrying poison to fangs

Many species of snakes have poison in their saliva. They have a pair of large teeth, called fangs, to inject the poison into their prey.

Weaverbird's nest

Boomslang snake

Boomslang snakes climb up acacia trees, snatch baby weaverbirds out of their nests and swallow them. They also take eggs from nests.

Weaverbird

Finding food

Snakes have poor eyesight and hearing, so they have to use other ways of finding their prey. They can feel vibrations from objects moving on the ground. They also pick up scents from the air or ground by flicking their forked tongues in and out. Some species, such as rattlesnakes, can sense tiny changes in temperature. This means they can tell if there is an animal nearby by the heat given off by its body.

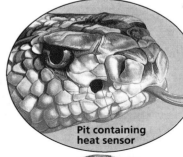

Pit containing heat sensor

On each side of their heads, rattlesnakes have a small pit that contains heat sensors. These help them sense changes in temperature.

This rattlesnake has sensed the heat given off by the body of a mouse.

The mouse tries to escape, but the snake follows it into its burrow.

The snake opens its mouth wide and strikes with its poisonous fangs.

After biting the mouse, the snake lets go and waits for the poison to work.

The mouse may wander away before dying but the snake finds it again.

Open wide

Snakes do not use their teeth to tear their prey apart. Instead, they swallow it whole. Most snakes can open their mouths very wide to eat food that is much larger than their heads. They do this by unhinging their upper and lower jaws. The skin on their necks and bodies stretches easily so large food fits inside. Snakes also produce lots of saliva to help food slide down.

African egg-eating snake

Egg-eating snakes swallow whole eggs. A row of sharp spines in the snake's throat pierces the shell. The snake swallows the egg's contents and spits out the broken shell.

Rock pythons coil their bodies around their prey to suffocate it. Then they swallow it head first. It may take them hours to swallow a large animal, and days to digest it. After a big meal, the snake may not eat again for months.

Rock python swallowing an impala

Baby snakes

A few species of snakes give birth to live babies, but most lay eggs with tough, leathery shells. They lay their eggs in shallow holes, cover them with a thin layer of soil and leave them to hatch. When the baby snakes hatch out, they have to look after themselves.

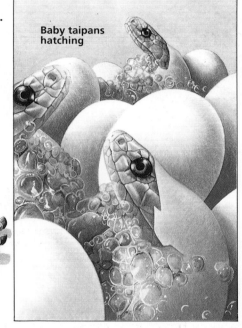

Baby taipans hatching

Warning signals

Several species of mammals and birds eat snakes. Instead of using their poison to attack an enemy immediately, many snakes give warning signals first. These may frighten the enemy into leaving them alone.

Rattlesnake's rattle

When a rattlesnake shakes the rattle at the end of its tail, it makes a loud rattling noise. The rattle is made up of interlocking sections of hard, dry skin.

As a threat, cobras raise the top part of their bodies off the ground and stretch the skin around their heads to make themselves look bigger.

Black-necked cobra

Milk snake

Coral snake

Milk snakes are harmless but they look very similar to poisonous coral snakes. Many enemies cannot tell the difference so they leave the milk snakes alone.

People in grasslands

Many groups of people live in grassland areas. For example, the Maasai people of East Africa have been living on the savanna for about 2,000 years. Today, some of them still live in small family groups and follow their traditional way of life. They keep herds of animals and get milk, meat, blood and skins from them. A Maasai group usually has two living areas, called bomas. They move from one to the other, depending on the season, so their animals always have fresh grass to eat.

The whole boma is surrounded by a fence of bushes or logs. Each family has its own entrance.

Fence

Entrance

Maasai houses are made of mud and dung, over a frame of poles. The doorways are narrow and there are no windows.

Inside the houses, it is quite dark. It is also smoky because the cooking is done on an open fire. The usual meal is a kind of milky porridge.

Each married woman lives in her own house with her children. Husbands often have more than one wife and visit them in turn.

Young animals are kept inside a small fenced area. Other animals wander freely around the boma.

The women milk the animals twice a day - once early in the morning and once in the evening. The milking takes over an hour.

Each morning, the men lead the animals out of the boma, to graze outside. They bring them in at night, so they are safe from predators.

The young men often perform exciting dances. They usually live outside the boma, only coming in for their meals.

The women fetch the firewood. They carry it on their backs and may have to walk 10km (over 6 miles) each day. They also fetch water.

This girl is dressed up for her wedding. Even on ordinary days, the women wear amazing beaded necklaces and earrings.

Farming

Today, most of the world's grasslands are used by farmers. They divide the land into fields and grow crops, such as wheat, rice and barley. They also keep animals, such as cattle, goats and sheep. Farming provides food for people, but is not always good for wild plants and animals.

Only grasses can grow well in fields where lots of farm animals feed. Other plants die if their top parts are always being eaten.

Coyote

Farmers used to kill coyotes to stop them from stealing their sheep. In some areas today, there are laws against killing coyotes.

Some of the things done by farmers are helpful to wildlife.

Wild plants have a chance to grow if farmers move their animals from field to field, leaving each field empty for part of the year.

Kori bustard waiting for insects

In Africa, farmers often burn areas of land, to grow new, green grass for their animals. Some species of birds wait at the edge of the fire, to catch insects escaping from the flames.

Danger from hunters

Many grassland animals have been hunted by people at one time or another. At first, they were hunted only by local people who depended on the animals to survive. Then outsiders moved in and began to hunt huge numbers of some species. They made money by selling skins from cheetahs, antelopes and snakes, horns from rhinos and feathers from ostriches. Some animals, such as bison and pronghorns, were hunted just for sport. Numbers got so low that some species were in danger of dying out, or becoming extinct. Today, there are laws protecting certain species but some people break the laws and go on hunting. This illegal hunting is called poaching.

There used to be 35 million guanacos but by the beginning of this century there were only about 500,000. Today, numbers have risen to over a million, because of protection.

Baby guanaco

Female guanaco

Guanacos live in three South American countries. In Chile and Peru, they are protected but in Argentina, they are still hunted for their meat, skins and wool.

The ivory trade

Ivory comes from elephants' tusks. For thousands of years, people have been carving things from it. Since the 17th century, huge amounts of African ivory has been sold to other countries. This is called the ivory trade. Elephants are killed just so that their tusks can be pulled out and sold. In 1989, 76 countries made an agreement to stop the ivory trade, but some elephants are still killed by poachers.

Ivory is mainly used to make ornaments and bracelets. Today, many people refuse to buy ivory things. They hope that if less ivory is sold, fewer elephants will be killed.

In 1989, the president of Kenya organized a huge bonfire of tusks confiscated from poachers, to show the world that the Kenyan government was against the ivory trade.

Animal tracking

People need to know about wildlife in order to protect it. Scientists working in grassland areas can learn about how animals live by following, or tracking, them. To do this, they put the animal to sleep for a short time and fit it with a collar which has a radio transmitter on it. The scientists can then pick up signals from the transmitter, using a receiver. When the animal wakes up, its movements can be tracked from a car or plane.

Black-footed ferrets are almost extinct. Most surviving ferrets have been fitted with radio collars, so scientists can keep track of them.

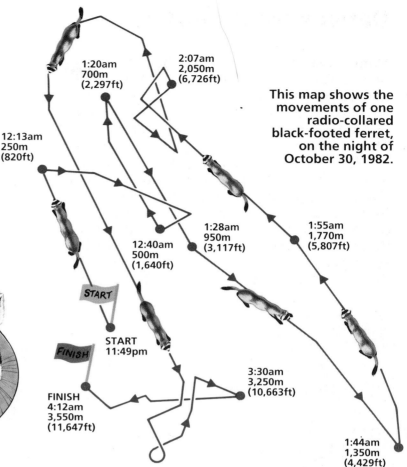

This map shows the movements of one radio-collared black-footed ferret, on the night of October 30, 1982.

1:20am
700m
(2,297ft)

2:07am
2,050m
(6,726ft)

12:13am
250m
(820ft)

1:28am
950m
(3,117ft)

1:55am
1,770m
(5,807ft)

12:40am
500m
(1,640ft)

START

START
11:49pm

FINISH

FINISH
4:12am
3,550m
(11,647ft)

3:30am
3,250m
(10,663ft)

1:44am
1,350m
(4,429ft)

African parks

Some African savanna areas have been made into huge parks or reserves. The animals are protected there and wardens try to stop poachers from getting in. Thousands of tourists visit these parks every year, to see the amazing wildlife. This brings money into the area and provides jobs for local people, but tourism can disturb wildlife if it is not properly controlled.

KENYA

There are over 50 parks and reserves in Kenya. They are shown in green on this map.

Cheetahs normally hunt during the day. In some areas, they have started hunting at night, so they are not disturbed by tourists in cars or vans.

Balloon rides over the savanna allow people to see the wildlife without disturbing it too much.

Index

Photograph of woman carrying firewood © WWF/John Newby
Photograph of young men dancing © Tony Souter/Hutchison Library
Photograph of girl dressed up for wedding © Steve Turner/Oxford Scientific Films
Photographs of cattle herders and of mother and child © Sean Sprague/Panos Pictures
Photographs of woman milking goat and of inside a Maasai house © Neil Cooper/Panos Pictures

To find out more about grassland animals, from rhinos to dung beetles, you could join LIFEWATCH, London Zoo's conservation group. People from all over the world can join. Address: Lifewatch, London Zoo, Regents Park, London NW1 4RY, UK.